Trouble at the Krusty Krab!

adapted by Steven Banks
illustrated by Zina Saunders
based on the movie written by Derek Drymon, Tim Hill, Steve Hillenburg,
Kent Osborne, Aaron Springer, and Paul Tibbitt

Ready-to-Read

Simon Spotlight/Nickelodeon
New York London Toronto Sydney

Based on *The SpongeBob SquarePants Movie* by Nickelodeon Movies and Paramount Pictures.

SIMON SPOTLIGHT
An imprint of Simon & Schuster Children's Publishing Division
1230 Avenue of the Americas, New York, New York 10020

Manufactured in the United States of America

First Edition
2 4 6 8 10 9 7 5 3 1

Library of Congress Cataloging-in-Publication Data
Banks, Steven, 1954-
Trouble at the Krusty Krab! / by Steven Banks.–1st ed.
p. cm. – (Ready-to-read)
"Based on the TV series SpongeBob SquarePants created by Stephen Hillenburg as seen on Nickelodeon."
Summary: When disaster hits the Krusty Krab, only SpongeBob SquarePants has what it takes to set things right.
ISBN 0-689-86838-3
[1. Marine animals–Fiction. 2. Restaurants–Fiction. 3. Humorous stories.] I. SpongeBob SquarePants (Television program) II. Title. III. Series.
PZ7.B22637Tro 2004 [E]–dc22 2003028066

There was trouble
at the Krusty Krab!
Police helicopters
circled above town.
The people of Bikini Bottom
had gathered to see
what was going on.

News reporters came up to
the owner, Mr. Krabs.
"The people want to know:
What is going on?"
asked a reporter.

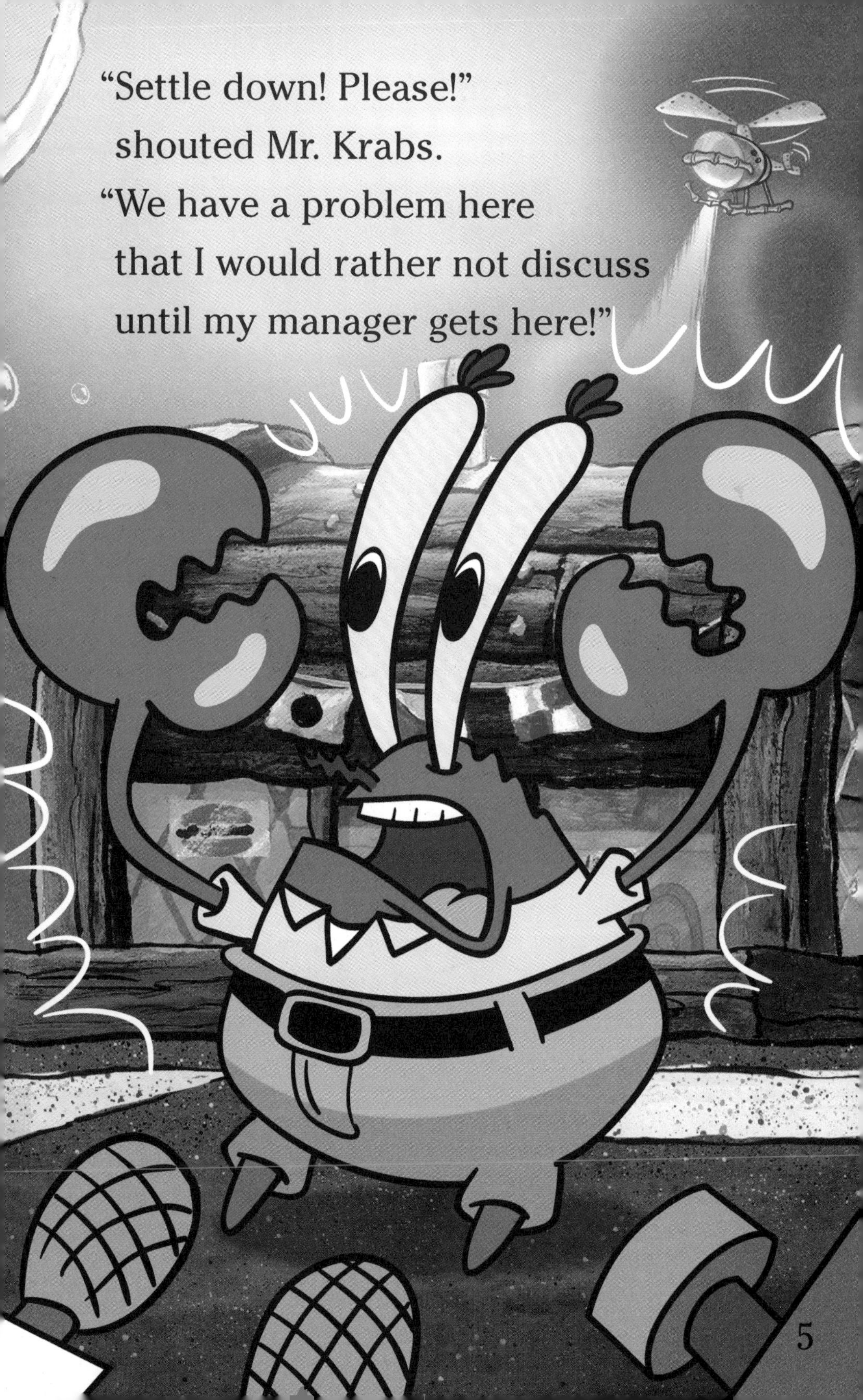

“Settle down! Please!”
shouted Mr. Krabs.
“We have a problem here
that I would rather not discuss
until my manager gets here!”

Just then a car pulled up,
and out stepped
SpongeBob SquarePants.
The crowd cheered!

"My manager is here!"
cried Mr. Krabs with a sigh
of relief. "The day is saved!
He will know what to do!"

"Talk to me, Krabs,"
said SpongeBob.
"It started out as a simple order:
a Krabby Patty with cheese,"
said Mr. Krabs.

"So what went wrong?"
asked SpongeBob.
"The customer took a bite
and . . . and . . . and . . ."
Mr. Krabs couldn't go on.

"Spit it out, Krabs!"
cried SpongeBob.
"THERE WAS NO CHEESE!"
shouted Mr. Krabs
as he started to cry.
"Get a hold of yourself, Eugene,"
cried SpongeBob.

SpongeBob faced the crowd.
"Okay, everyone," said SpongeBob,
"I am going in."
Patrick ran up to SpongeBob
and begged, "Do not do it!
It's too dangerous!"
SpongeBob smiled. "Do not worry.
'Dangerous' is my middle name!"

As SpongeBob walked up
to the door he said,
"If I do not make it back alive,
give all my jellyfishing nets
to Squidward."
"I do not want them!"
yelled Squidward from the crowd.

The crowd watched as SpongeBob entered the Krusty Krab.

"Will SpongeBob be able to get some cheese on that patty, Mr. Krabs?" asked a reporter.

"He has to! He must!" said Mr. Krabs.
"But what if he can't?"
asked the reporter.
"THEN THE WORLD AS WE KNOW IT
IS OVER!" cried Mr. Krabs.

The customer who had
ordered the Krabby Patty sat
in the corner of the restaurant.
He looked up at SpongeBob.
"Who are you?" he asked.
"I am the manager of this place,"
said SpongeBob.

“I am really scared, man!”
cried the customer.
SpongeBob replied, “Do not worry.
Everything is going to be fine.”

Outside, the crowd waited.
A reporter spoke into a microphone
saying, "SpongeBob has been
inside for ten seconds!"
"The suspense is killing me!"
cried Mr. Krabs.
"Me too," said Patrick,
eating an ice-cream cone.

ack inside, SpongeBob sat down with
he customer. "Do you have a name?"
sked SpongeBob.

My name is Phil," said the customer.

SpongeBob nodded and said,
That's a good name."

"YOU DO NOT UNDERSTAND!"
screamed Phil.
"I CANNOT TAKE IT! THERE WAS
NO CHEESE!"

"Stay with me, Phil!"
said SpongeBob.
"Do you have a family?"
"Yes," replied Phil.
"I have a lovely wife
and two great children."
"That's what it is all about,"
said SpongeBob.

“Okay, Phil,” said SpongeBob.
“Stay calm. I am just going to
open my briefcase.”
“Why?” cried Phil.
“I have only got one shot at this,
and I have to get out the
right tools for the job,”
said SpongeBob.

SpongeBob reached into the briefcase and pulled out a pair of solid gold tweezers.

"Solid gold tweezers!" shouted Phil.

"Yes, they are!" said SpongeBob.

“Now I want you to do me
a favor, Phil,”
said SpongeBob.
“What?” Phil asked.
“Say cheese!” said
SpongeBob as he pulled
out a slice of . . .
CHEESE!

SpongeBob carefully put the cheese onto the Krabby Patty.

Success! The cheese was on the Krabby Patty!

SpongeBob marched out of the Krusty Krab with a smiling Phil by his side.

"Order up!" cried SpongeBob.

"SpongeBob, I would like to give you the Manager of the Year Award!" said Mr. Krabs. SpongeBob just smiled back, looking pleased with himself.

Then Mr. Krabs turned to Phil and said, "And that will be two dollars and ninety-five cents for the Krabby Patty, Phil."

Suddenly the crowd gathered around SpongeBob and lifted him up in the air.

"Three cheers for the manager!" cried Mr. Krabs. "Hip hip!"

Honk!

"Hip, hip!" shouted Mr. Krabs.

Honk!

Honk!

"What's that noise?"
wondered SpongeBob.

"Sounds like an alarm clock
going off to me," said Patrick.

"It's my alarm clock!"
said SpongeBob.

"I must be dreaming!"

SpongeBob woke up in his bed.

"Gary, I had my favorite dream again about being the manager of the Krusty Krab! Do you think it will ever happen, Gary?"

"Meow," said Gary.

SpongeBob smiled.

"That is exactly how I feel!"